Welcome to ALADDIN QUIX!

If you are looking for fast, fun-to-read stories with colorful characters, lots of kid-friendly humor, easy-to-follow action, entertaining story lines, and lively illustrations, then **ALADDIN QUIX** is for you!

But wait, there's more!

If you're also looking for stories with tables of contents; word lists; about-the-book questions; 64, 80, or 96 pages; short chapters; short paragraphs; and large fonts, then **ALADDIN QUIX** is *definitely* for you!

ALADDIN QUIX: The next step between ready to reads and longer, more challenging chapter books, for readers five to eight years old.

Mini Mermaid Tales

Read more ALADDIN QUIX books!

By Stephanie Calmenson

Our Principal Is a Frog!
Our Principal Is a Wolf!
Our Principal's in His Underwear!
Our Principal Breaks a Spell!
Our Principal's Wacky Wishes!

Royal Sweets
By Helen Perelman

Book 1: *A Royal Rescue*
Book 2: *Sugar Secrets*
Book 3: *Stolen Jewels*
Book 4: *The Marshmallow Ghost*
Book 5: *Chocolate Challenge*

A Miss Mallard Mystery
By Robert Quackenbush

Dig to Disaster
Texas Trail to Calamity
Express Train to Trouble
Stairway to Doom
Bicycle to Treachery
Gondola to Danger
Surfboard to Peril
Taxi to Intrigue

Little Goddess Girls
By Joan Holub and Suzanne Williams

Book 1: *Athena & the Magic Land*
Book 2: *Persephone & the Giant Flowers*
Book 3: *Aphrodite & the Gold Apple*
Book 4: *Artemis & the Awesome Animals*
Book 5: *Athena & the Island Enchantress*
Book 6: *Persephone & the Evil King*
Book 7: *Aphrodite & the Magical Box*
Book 8: *Artemis & the Wishing Kitten*

Mini Mermaid Tales

The Friendship Wish

by Debbie Dadey

Illustrated by Fuuji Takashi

Q QUIX

ALADDIN QUIX

New York   London   Toronto   Sydney   New Delhi

ALADDIN QUIX
Simon & Schuster Children's Publishing Division
1230 Avenue of the Americas, New York, New York 10020
First Aladdin QUIX paperback edition May 2023
Text copyright © 2023 by Debbie Dadey
Illustrations copyright © 2023 by Fuuji Takashi
Also available in an Aladdin QUIX hardcover edition.
All rights reserved, including the right of reproduction in whole or in part in any form.
ALADDIN and the related marks and colophon are trademarks
of Simon & Schuster, Inc.
For information about special discounts for bulk purchases, please contact
Simon & Schuster Special Sales at 1-866-506-1949 or
business@simonandschuster.com.
The Simon & Schuster Speakers Bureau can bring authors to your live event. For more
information or to book an event contact the Simon & Schuster Speakers Bureau
at 1-866-248-3049 or visit our website at www.simonspeakers.com.
Designed by Karin Paprocki & Evelyn Wang
The illustrations for this book were rendered digitally.
The text of this book was set in Archer Medium.
Manufactured in the United States of America 0323 OFF
2 4 6 8 10 9 7 5 3 1
CIP data for this book is available from the Library of Congress.
ISBN 9781534489257 (hc)
ISBN 9781534489240 (pbk)
ISBN 9781534489264 (ebook)

To Ada

Cast of Characters

Rosie: Mergirl who is new to Trident City

Aqua: Mergirl who is Rosie's first friend

Rocky: Rosie's older cousin

Headmaster Hermit: Principal at Trident Academy

Nanny Manny: Nanny who takes care of Rosie

Mom: Rosie's mother

Dad: Rosie's father

Freddie: New friend from Mini Mermaids and Merboys

Poppy: New friend from Mini Mermaids and Merboys

Contents

Chapter 1: Rosie Meets Aqua   1

Chapter 2: School Trip   10

Chapter 3: Caught!   20

Chapter 4: Super Bubbles   29

Chapter 5: A Big Surprise   37

Chapter 6: Rosie's New School   48

Word List   57

Questions   61

1

Rosie Meets Aqua

Rosie's nose itched. Her rosy red tail itched too. She wanted to sing her favorite shark song. But she didn't move. She didn't sing. She was like a **statue** in her front yard.

Rosie was trying to be still enough to catch a fish. After all, fish like school. And Rosie really, really wanted to play school with someone. Her cousin Rocky lived next door and went to Trident Academy, but Rosie was only seven. She was still a year *too* young.

Just then, a tiny shrimp **nibbled** on the end of Rosie's long pink hair. She wiggled, but the shrimp kept chewing. "Please stop. You're too little to play school," Rosie whispered. "You'll mess up everything."

Luckily, the shrimp floated away. Just in time! A big fish was coming Rosie's way. *One. Two. Three.* **Grab!**

Rosie caught the yellow fish's tail. But then the fish **puffed** up into a big pointy ball. **Yikes!**

Rosie let go super fast. "**Ouch!** That hurts! That was very rude!" Rosie called as the yellow fish zipped away, leaving her with a sore finger.

"What were you doing with that porcupine fish?" A mergirl with her hair pulled into two braids swam up to Rosie. Her tail was a swirl of blue and green. Rosie had never seen anything like it. Her

own tail was bright red with zig-zags.

"Who are you?" Rosie asked.

The mergirl put her hands on her hips. "I'm **Aqua**, but you shouldn't hurt a fish."

"I didn't!" Rosie held up her red finger. "It hurt me. I was just trying to get it to play school."

"Oh," Aqua said. "May I play instead?"

"Yes!" Rosie twirled in a circle. She loved dancing, almost as much as she loved playing school.

She had been hoping to find a friend ever since she'd moved to Trident City three days ago.

"But there's just one problem. I've never played school before. Do you know how?"

Aqua **shrugged**. "I've never played either. But I could ask my older sister, Shira. She goes to Trident Academy. We live over there." Aqua pointed to a bright orange house that was only two shells behind where Rosie lived with her mother, father, and Nanny Manny.

Rosie's parents often had to travel for their Angel Fish Antiques store, so Nanny Manny took care of her. Right now Nanny was making crab cookies.

"**Rocky** goes there too," Rosie said. "And there he is."

A dark-haired merboy with a purple tail zipped out of the house next door. He was racing after a group of merkids on their way to Trident Academy.

"I've seen him before," Aqua said. "He's *always* late for school."

Rosie nodded. "That sounds like Rocky. I wish I could go with him and see what a real school looks like."

Aqua smiled. "Why don't we?"

2

School Trip

"I don't know if we should," Rosie said, biting her lip.

Aqua said, "We're just going to take a quick look. I've never been inside."

As long as they only peeked,

it would be okay. Rosie would be back home before Nanny was done with the crab cookies. "Let's hurry," Rosie said.

As quick as sailfish, they swam after Rocky. But as they caught up to a group of students headed toward Trident Academy, the small mergirls were swept through the huge school door with them!

Oh no! Rosie couldn't believe it! They weren't supposed to actually go in.

"Now what do we do?" Rosie asked Aqua. "We have to get out of here before we get into deep-sea trouble!"

"Don't worry, Rosie. It will be all right. Like I said, we'll just take a quick look around. Then we'll know how to play school ourselves."

As the students swam to their classrooms, Aqua headed down

the hallway with Rosie close
behind.

"Rosie, come see this!" Aqua
swam into a big room filled with
sea **scrolls** and kelp books. "Look

at all these stories," she squealed. "I want to read them all!"

"Shhh, someone might hear you," Rosie whispered. What if they said Rosie could never come back to school, even when she was old enough?

"Let's see what else they have here." Aqua grinned.

"Stop!" Rosie hissed. "We should go home. Now!"

But Aqua was already gone! Rosie **peered** out into the hall just as Aqua's blue-and-green tail

slipped into another room. Rosie
dashed after her.

Rosie couldn't believe her
eyes. One side of the new room
was filled with paints, clay, kelp

paper, and paintbrushes. The other part of the room had drums, guitarfish, banjo rays, and trumpet fish for making music. Rosie's dad played the guitarfish and was going to teach Rosie how to play. It was her favorite instrument!

Aqua banged on a large drum before blowing into a trumpet fish.

"*Shhh*, Aqua. We need to be quiet!" Rosie pulled the trumpet fish away from her.

But it was too late. Voices came

from out in the hallway. Were they getting closer?

Rosie's heart pounded. How could they **escape**?

What if Aqua got her into big trouble? Maybe Rosie *shouldn't* be friends with her. . . .

"We'll go soon, Rosie," Aqua said. "I just want to check out the paints. I've never seen such a pretty pink before." Aqua held up a huge jar and . . .

Splash!

The pink paint landed all over

Rosie's red tail, on her face, and even on her favorite dolphin T-shirt.

"Oops," Aqua said. "Sorry about that."

Suddenly, a very angry voice snapped, "What are you two doing in here?"

3

Caught!

As Rosie and Aqua quietly fol-
lowed **Headmaster Hermit**
through the crowded hallway,
someone called Rosie's name.

It was Rocky! **Yikes!**

"Rosie! What are you doing

in school?" her cousin shouted. "You're not supposed to be here."

Rosie was in trouble with a capital *T*. Rocky would tell her parents. She would be stuck at home forever!

"Please take a seat in my office," the headmaster told them. "I will be right back."

Headmaster Hermit's office was filled with books and students' artwork. His desk was covered with papers, a sea quill pen, and a coral name tag.

"Rosie, I'm sorry," Aqua **apologized**. "I was having so much fun, I didn't want to stop."

Rosie didn't **utter** a sound, but her tail was shaking. What would happen now?

Headmaster Hermit glided into

his office and sat at his desk.

"So, merkids," the headmaster began, "would you like to tell me what you were doing in the music and art room? I know all my students, and I don't **recall** ever seeing the two of you."

Aqua looked at Rosie. Rosie looked at Aqua.

"Well, we, uh . . . we, uh, well," Aqua said.

Then Rosie **blurted** out, "We wanted to see Trident Academy so we would know how to play school. We've never been, and it looks like fun!"

Headmaster Hermit nodded and left once again. "I'll be right back."

Nanny Manny was happy. Usually. She loved teaching Rosie everything about ocean tides, angelfish, and even glowing fish. But she was not happy when she came to take Rosie home from Trident Academy.

And she was not happy when Rosie left a trail of pink paint on the clean floor of their shell.

And Nanny Manny was really not happy when she was worried. "I was so worried about you, Rosie. How could you leave home without telling me?"

Nanny was right. Rosie had been wrong.

"I'm so, so sorry, Nanny. I didn't mean to scare you, but Aqua and I were swept up into Trident

Academy by the other students.
Once we were there, we just
wanted to look around a little bit."

Nanny Manny put her hands
on her hips. "You were gone a

long time. Why did you go?"

Rosie bowed her head. "I wanted to see a *real* school. And Aqua was the first friend I've made since we moved here. I love you, Nanny, but I miss merkids my own age."

"Well, make sure you never ever do that again," Nanny Manny said, wiping a tear from her eye.

Rosie held up a hand. "I promise."

Nanny Manny pointed to the

bathroom. "Now go wash your tail before your parents get home."

Oh no! Rosie had a feeling her day of trouble wasn't over yet.

4

Super Bubbles

Rosie raced into the bathroom. Her tail had lots and lots of pink dots and **splotches** on it. Rosie liked pink, but the paint was itchy! A quick rub with a cloth didn't work. Maybe soap would help. To make sure she was extra clean, Rosie poured out lots of soap. And then a bit more just to make sure.

Bubbles covered her tail. Bubbles covered her arms, her neck, and the tip of her chin. Soon the whole bathroom filled with bubbles. **"Super bubbles!"** Rosie yelled.

"Rosie!" Nanny Manny rushed into the bathroom and frowned at the mountain of suds. "Young lady, that is quite enough."

"Oops. I guess I used too much soap," Rosie giggled.

But Nanny wasn't laughing. She wasn't happy. Again!

"I'll clean it up right away," Rosie said quickly.

Nanny Manny said, "And after you **tidy** this, your room is next. Your parents will be home soon, and I want everything in order."

Bubbles aren't easy to clean up. When Rosie popped them, she made an even bigger mess.

When she was finally done in

the bathroom, Rosie floated into her messy bedroom. It would be easier to clean if Aqua helped. It might even be fun, but she was probably in trouble too.

When Aqua's dad picked her up from school, he was just as upset as Nanny Manny. Would Rosie ever see Aqua again? Even though they had done something wrong, Rosie hoped they'd get another chance at being friends. And playing school.

"Maybe I could hide the mess

and clean it later," Rosie said.

Zip! Her dolls and balls went on her bed.

Zip! She tossed her cover on top. Her bed was just a tiny bit bumpy.

Zip! Her clothes went into the bottom of her closet. Only a few stuck out when she closed the door.

Zip! She hid a cookie plate and cup behind a toy dolphin. She swept her artwork under the bed. Was there anything left?

Zip! She took the small rug beside her bed and threw it over her rock collection.

"Are you finished cleaning your room, Rosie?" Nanny called to her.

Rosie **studied** her work. Nanny Manny wouldn't like it. It wasn't a good job at all. It would only add to the trouble Rosie was already in.

"Not yet, Nanny," Rosie answered. Then she dove in and really started tidying up, one book, one rock, one toy at a time.

Just as she folded the last shirt, she heard her mother's voice. **"Rosie! We're home.** Please come here right away."

Uh-oh!

5

A Big Surprise

Rosie froze.

She wanted to hide in her closet or under her bed. But she knew if she didn't go to her parents, they would come to her.

Rosie swam into the living

room where her parents and Nanny Manny were talking. None of them looked happy. Before her parents could **fuss** at her, Rosie said quickly, "I'm so sorry.

I shouldn't have gone to Trident Academy with Aqua."

Mom nodded.

Dad nodded.

Nanny Manny nodded.

Rosie's tailed twitched and twitched. What else could she say?

"I didn't have anyone to play school with. I'm too young to go to the Academy with Rocky. Aqua and I were only going to take a quick peek inside, but—"

Nanny stopped her. "Rosie, please put on a sweater. It's getting colder. We don't want to be late."

Late for what? Rosie wondered.

"We are going somewhere that will keep you from getting into trouble," Rosie's dad told her.

Rosie gulped. Where could they be going? A clamshell jail for merkids? A deep-sea dungeon?

Together they floated away from the house. First they glided past a huge hammerhead shark statue, then over a field of kelp, and then around the Great White Whale Museum. The farther they

went from Rosie's house, the more she worried.

Finally, they arrived at a bright yellow shell.

Her mom pointed to a big sign and read aloud: "'Mini Mermaids and Merboys.'"

Rosie's stomach dropped. Was this the deep-sea dungeon?

"Rosie," Mom said, smiling broadly. "Welcome to your new school."

"A school? For me? You mean this isn't a dungeon?"

"A dungeon?" Dad asked. "What are you talking about? Are you playing pretend?"

"Uh, um, uh . . . ," Rosie **stammered**.

"We know you are sorry for this morning," Nanny Manny said.

"And," Dad said, "it will never happen again. Right, Rosie?"

Rosie really was sorry. "I promise."

Then Rosie heard laughing. Merkids were swimming back

and forth around the benches in
front of the school—and they all
looked her age!

A merboy with a striped tail sat
on a rock looking at a kelp book.
One mergirl had a tail that wasn't

just blue or just green. It was a mix of colors. She was far away, but she looked like Aqua! Another mergirl had swirls on her bright yellow fins.

Rosie grinned. She enjoyed books as much as she loved playing school, dancing, and singing. Maybe some of these merkids would want to play school.

The Mini Mermaid and Merboy School looked way more fun than playing with a porcupine fish!

"Today we are visiting to see if we like it," Mom explained.

"We can meet your teacher if you do," Dad added.

"I like it!" Rosie cheered. **"It's fin-tastic!"**

6

Rosie's New School

"You can join the merkids if you'd like," Nanny Manny said.

Rosie watched everyone playing. She really wanted to say hello, but there were so many of them. "I am a tiny bit scared," she whispered.

Mom patted Rosie's back. "Would you like me to go with you?"

Rosie shook her head. **"No, I can do this."**

Rosie floated toward the merboy reading a book. She got closer and closer. Before she could say a word, he looked up and said, "Do you know this story? *Whale Tale Adventures*?"

Rosie nodded. Rocky had shown her that book.

Then the merboy asked, "Do you like playing tuna tag? Do you like playing with blue clay? Do you like playing school?"

Rosie's heart pounded. She nodded again and again and again.

"My name is **Freddie**." Then he shouted, "Aqua! **Poppy**!"

Was he calling someone? Could Aqua be the same mergirl she knew? "What's a poppy?"

Freddie grinned. "Not *what*. Who." Two mergirls rushed over to them.

Freddie pointed to the one with

the blue-and-green tail. "That's Aqua."

Rosie didn't know what to do. Should she be mad at Aqua for getting her into trouble? Would Aqua be mad at her?

"I already know Aqua," Rosie told Freddie. "Hi," she said, looking **shyly** at the other mergirl.

Aqua put her hands behind her back. "I'm sorry about this morning."

Rosie answered, "Well, I didn't have to go." She had known better.

"I'm glad the headmaster told my dad about this place," Aqua said. "It looks like fun, doesn't it?"

The other mergirl with the swirls on her bright yellow tail called out, "My name is Poppy!"

"Guess what?" Freddie said. "Rosie likes to play school."

Poppy squealed, and Aqua clapped her hands.

"Do you think we can play school right now?" Rosie asked.

No one said anything for a minute, and then Freddie

answered, "I get to be the teacher first!"

"I'm next!" Poppy called.

Freddie laughed. "I hope you don't mind. Sometimes we are a little loud."

If being loud was part of playing school, then Rosie didn't mind one bit.

Aqua added, "As long as everyone gets a turn at being teacher, Freddie."

Aqua started giggling and did a backwards flip.

"It's time to play," Freddie said, smiling at the new students. "This is the word 'sand,'" he told them, **tracing** the word in the sand with his finger. "Now you each write it five times."

Rosie slowly wrote the word. So did Poppy and Aqua.

When Rosie finished, she looked around the schoolyard. Her parents and Nanny were talking to some other parents. Some merkids lined up for the shell slide, and others zoomed around playing tuna tag.

Rosie couldn't believe her luck. This day had turned from awful to **awesome**. Surely, with three new friends and a school of her own, she'd never get into deep-sea trouble ever again. Rosie was so happy she twirled in a circle. She loved playing school and dancing, but now she had something new to love—friends!

Word List

apologized (uh•POL•uh•jyzed):
Said sorry

awesome (AW•sum): Really good,
wonderful

blurted (BLUR•ted): Said something
quickly without thought

escape (eh•SKAYP): Get away, get free

fuss (FUHS): To give attention that
is not wanted

nibbled (NIH•buld): Gently bit

peered (PEERD): Looked curiously
at something

puffed (PUFT): Blew up with air

recall (rih•CAHL): Remember

scrolls (SKROHLS): Rolls of paper used to draw or write on

shrugged (SHRUHGD): Raised one's shoulders

shyly (SHY•lee): Quietly

splotches (SPLAH•chiz): Messy spots or stains

stammered (STAM•erd): Spoke in a halting, slow way

statue (STA•choo): Art made from stone, metal, or other hard material

studied (STUH•deed): Looked at something closely

tidy (TY•dee): Clean up

tracing (TRAY•sing): Copying by following lines of a shape

utter (UH•ter): Say a word or sound

Questions

1. How many days have Rosie and her family lived in Trident City?
2. Do you think Rosie would have gone into Trident Academy if she and Aqua hadn't been swept inside with the other students? Would you have?
3. What instrument does Rosie's father play? Why do you think it's Rosie's favorite?
4. What is the name of Rosie's parents' store?

5. What do Freddie and Rosie both like to do besides play school?

6. Rosie loves playing school and dancing. What are two things that you love to do? Do you have a friend who likes to do those things?